E3⁰⁰

W9-BRN-419

KEMI

3769

K E M I

AN INDIAN BOY BEFORE
THE WHITE MAN CAME

MARY AND CONRAD BUFF

THE WARD RITCHIE PRESS

DEDICATED TO
BERNICE EASTMAN JOHNSTON

Without whose help and
constant belief this book would
never have been written.

COPYRIGHT © 1966 BY MARY MARSH BUFF AND CONRAD BUFF
FIRST PRINTING SEPTEMBER 1966
SECOND PRINTING JUNE 1968
LIBRARY OF CONGRESS CARD NUMBER 66-16256
DESIGNED BY JOSEPH SIMON
LITHOGRAPHED IN THE UNITED STATES OF AMERICA
BY ANDERSON, RITCHIE & SIMON

Cyn Hls

EXPLANATION

THE STORY OF KEMI of the stone age is the story of countless other Kemis who once lived in a pleasant land later called California.

Fifty years after Columbus found the new world, another explorer, Cabrillo, sailed along the Pacific coast. Hugging rocky shores for days and days. He believed he had found a great island.

Cabrillo's white-sailed ships looked like great white birds to the simple Indians when his boats found shelter in a harbor on Catalina Island. They were friendly and helpful to the strange white men whom they thought *might* be gods.

Not much is really known about the Indians of California. They had no written language. But scientists and students year by year piece together bits of knowledge here—there.

This is much like finding an old book in the attic of an ancient house. Many of the pages of the book may be missing. Many of the pages may be torn. Others may be faded with age or eaten by insects.

Our knowledge of the Indians is much the same. But, from what we can piece together, we learn that the Indians of California were a happy people little given to warfare. They were a people who lived in a mild climate and beautiful land. Here nature was generous and gave them the food they needed for all months of the year.

CYNTHIA HEIGHTS SCHOOL
EVANSVILLE, INDIANA

TABLE OF CONTENTS

THE AMERICAN INDIANS

A long, long time ago
Thousands of years ago
Before the peoples of Europe
Knew of the New World
Indians lived in the Americas

Centuries before
Wandering hunters had struggled
Over a narrow strip of frozen land
In the far north
Where Asia and America joined

They wandered
In small groups
And at different times
Carrying
Spears
Throwing sticks
And followed by their hunting dogs

Some Indians drifted south
And southeast
Where it was warmer
Always following game
They drifted as far as the very tip
Of South America

Others remained
Where food was plentiful
Families became clans
Clans grew into tribes
Tribes became nations

In new settlements
The people found new foods
They created new tools
Then someone
At some unknown time
Created the greatest of all tools —
The bow and arrow

Along the coast
Of the great Pacific Ocean
Indians lived
On gifts from the sea
Fish
Shellfish
Otter
Seals

But Inland
Among rolling hills
In a land the Spanish later called
California
The Indians lived on acorns
And small game
A happy people
In a pleasant land
Until
In the Sixteenth Century
Explorers came
In great white-sailed ships
To change their lives forever

CHAPTER 1: THE BROKEN BOWL

IT WAS OCTOBER in the Village among the Willows which lay at the foot of a great mountain. This was the month the Indians called "the time when we grow fat." For now the acorns ripened everywhere on the many oak trees in the valleys. The Indians lived mainly on mush made from acorns.

Kemi sat on the ground near his round rush-covered hut. It was one in an Indian village of some forty huts, all alike.

Most of the Indians of the village were busy at something. Father and some friends were tanning deerskins. Mother had gone away with other women to find seeds, herbs, and roots to flavor acorn mush and rabbit stew.

Grandfather, who was very old, had been a great messenger when he was young. He had carried messages from his village to others as he was a fast runner and had a fine memory. Just now he was resting in the sweathouse nearby.

Grandmother weaving a basket was hidden behind

3

the hut. When she was young she had been famous for her beautiful baskets. Now that she was old and could not see well she did not make many baskets.

Kemi sat alone on the ground smoothing a rabbit stick he had just made with a piece of rough sandstone. Rabbit sticks had to be very smooth.

Wusi, his dog, who was half coyote, lay beside him. Wusi *seemed* to be asleep. His eyes were closed. Suddenly he opened his eyes, pricked up his ears and sniffed. Kemi looked up. He saw something move under a bush. A rabbit!

Without thinking he threw his curved stick at the rabbit. It missed. It struck a storage bin. As it bounced back Kemi heard a loud noise. The stick had hit Mother's fine stone cooking pot. The pot lay in pieces near the ashes of an outdoor fire. It was still warm enough to cook out of doors in this pleasant land.

The pot was not just an *ordinary* pot. Most Indian women cooked mush in rough old granite pots. Mother treasured this stone pot more than anything she owned except her shining shell necklaces. Stone pots like the one Kemi had just broken were hard to get.

Kemi knew that many years ago when Grandfather was a village messenger he had gone to the ocean two or three days' journey westward. He had brought back this pot to Grandmother. He told her then that it was made by the People of the Mountains in the Sea. These Indians lived on a great island which many centuries later the Spaniards named Santa Catalina.

Only the people on this island carved stone bowls like Mother's. The reason was that they had a secret ledge of soft rock we call soapstone on their island. They carved many things from soapstone—pipes, ornaments, and small copies of animals they knew, such as whales and the much-beloved porpoise. They believed that the porpoise was more human than animal and guarded their world from harm.

But of all the things the people of the island carved, their pots were the most valuable. They carried these pots in great boats, to the people who lived along the sea coasts. They traded with them for things which they needed for themselves.

Kemi stared at the pieces of broken bowl and was very sad. He glanced around to see if anyone might have seen him. Everybody was busy working elsewhere.

What should he do now? Should he tell Mother when she came home? Should he tell Father? Would Father punish him? Indians seldom punished their children. But would Father tell the Headman? Would the Headman tell the Medicine Man?

Kemi imagined all kinds of frightful things that might happen to him. He feared most of all the Medicine Man. Was he a *real* man? Or was he a bear? Was he a wizard? Everyone in the village feared him; Father, Mother, Grandmother, and even his dear old Grandfather. Even *they* did not know if he were man or wizard.

The Medicine Man knew about herbs and plants that would cure people. Sometimes he sucked an evil spirit from people that made them sick. It was even whispered that he might kill people if he did not like them. No one in the village questioned his power.

Kemi stared at the bits of broken bowl but dared not cry. Then he hurriedly ran to his favorite hiding place in an old sycamore tree that grew near the river. Wusi followed.

As Kemi climbed the great trunk of the tree to his hiding place, Wusi whined. He tried to climb too, but of course he always slipped down.

A gray squirrel who lived in the tree barked at Kemi. Blue jays screamed at him as he hid in his secret place between two great limbs. As he peered out between autumn leaves he saw everyone who moved in the village. Now that nobody could *see* tears rolled down his brown cheeks.

The unhappy boy wondered how he could ever get another cooking pot like the one he had just broken. He knew he must trade something for one. But he had nothing to trade. All he owned was a little leather bag in which he kept a few colored stones he had found and a few bright birds' feathers.

As the Indian boy hid in his secret perch, frightened and alone, the sun slipped downward toward the earth. The Indians believed the great sun saw everything that went on in the world.

Now Kemi saw Grandfather stumble from the sweat

house wiping his face. To think that Grandfather had once been a great runner and a village messenger! He watched Father and an uncle carry cured deerskins and put them in a pile.

Soon Father would lead a few village men westward to the ocean to trade these skins for things the village people needed. He went every year. For Father, too, had been a messenger when he was young. He knew the country for miles and miles.

The rugged mountain looming behind the village slowly changed to pink. The sun was almost gone. Squirrels stopped barking. Even the noisy blue jays were quiet. It was time to rest. Then Kemi saw Mother straggling home with the baby on her back. Her basket was *always* full of leaves and herbs. Nona, Kemi's little sister, straggled along with her.

Suddenly Kemi heard a shrill cry. Mother had *seen* the broken pot. Now Grandfather, Grandmother, and Father gathered about her. Kemi could hear their excited voices. He heard Mother cry out once again.

As he watched his unlucky family in the golden glow of the setting sun he had never been so unhappy. Once more he wondered, "Shall I tell Father? Shall I tell Mother?" But each time the vision of the Medicine Man as he often saw him, dressed in a bear robe, frightened him. No, he could not tell them. Not *now* anyway. He would have to wait until he could think more.

Kemi smelled the smoke of supper fires. He was hungry. Wusi whined. He wanted to go home. As it grew

dark, bats darted through the air chasing flying insects. The pink mountains became dark and gloomy. A star came out. The Indians believed stars were the spirits of great men who had died and now lived in the sky.

Quietly Kemi slid down the trunk of the tree. He drifted like a shadow toward home. In the dusk no one noticed him. When he reached home he squatted behind his family. *Still* no one noticed him. Children always sat behind their elders around the fire. That was the custom.

Mother was trying to cook acorn mush in an old granite pot. She had not used this pot for years. It was very rough inside and hard to clean even with a stiff yucca brush. Sometimes the mush tasted moldy. Father did not like moldy mush.

At last the mush was ready. Father dipped a shell into it and supped the mush. So did all the others. As Kemi ate he watched his mother in the flickering light of the evening fire. Her cheeks were streaked with tears. No one spoke.

Night had come. A coyote yipped from a distant hill, sounding like many coyotes. An owl hooted from a tree. Some Indians believed the hoot of an owl meant that death was near for someone. Grandfather pulled his rabbit skin cape about his old bent shoulders. In this southern land the nights were often chilly. The days were usually warm. No one needed much clothing.

After eating Kemi crept inside the hut. He lay down

on his own reed mat, his feet toward the center. He looked up through the smoke hole at the top of the hut where the smoke of winter fires went out. The night was clear. He could see stars and stars and stars.

He heard Grandmother stumble in and lie on her mat beside him. He was so quiet that Grandmother asked, "Are you well, my grandson?"

The boy answered, "Yes Grandmother, I am well. But I was watching the stars, the great men, the Ancients."

They were both silent for awhile. Then Kemi asked, "Grandmother, won't you tell me *again* the story of how our people first came into this land many years ago?"

Grandmother seemed to know that Kemi was troubled. He often talked to her about his troubles more than to his mother. It seemed Mother was always so busy pounding acorns, weaving and cooking.

Grandmother cleared her throat and said, "It is an old, old story. You have heard it many times before as we sit around the fire when it is cold. But I will tell it to you again. Perhaps I will not remember just as I told it before. Sometimes I forget. I am old, my grandson."

Kemi answered, "I like to hear it *always*, Grandmother. I will listen, listen. You tell good stories."

She began, "This happened a long time ago. No one alive really knows *when* it happened. This story has come down to us from the Ancients. Once our people were wandering in a far off land. They were hungry

16

and thirsty and without any leader. They were lost.

They wandered and wandered. Many of them died of thirst and hunger. And then one among them became a leader. He said, "Let us go toward the setting sun." They followed because they trusted him. They came to a place between two mountains. They were cold and hungry. They had nothing to keep them warm. Many days later this great leader led them into this pleasant land below the great mountains where we live now peacefully."

Kemi sighed. He loved to hear this old story. He asked, "Grandmother, what was the name of this great leader?" Of course he knew it.

Grandmother replied, "The people called him Wyot. Wyot was wise. He taught the people what foods were good to eat and what foods were not good to eat. He showed them the plants that were poison. From him they learned how to make the bitter acorns sweet. Our people flourished.

"In this fair land of ours they killed rabbits, squirrels and deer. For they knew the bow and arrow. But then Wyot grew old. The people carried him from place to place, hoping to make him well again. But at last he died.

The time came to cremate him, as was the custom. His spirit ascended to the sky. He became the moon—the kindly moon that looks down upon us every month. The moon we love and trust."

The boy listened to this lovely old story as his grandmother always told it in a different way. It was *ever* new.

"Grandmother," he confided, "when the new moon rises each month, the old men light fires. As the boys run races in honor of Wyot, I race too. And, Grandmother, I often am the first one to finish."

Grandmother said, "So I hear, my grandson—that you are as fleet as the deer. You run like the wind. Perhaps, someday, you may be a messenger too as were your grandfather and your father."

Kemi was comforted. He had forgotten about the broken bowl. He did not hear the others as they came to bed. He was sound asleep.

But Kemi woke early the next morning before dawn. The birds were chirping outside in the trees as they always do. He slipped out of the hut quietly and ran down to the river to bathe. The Indians bathed before the sun came up. They feared the sun as the sun saw everything that was done on earth.

The water was cold. Kemi shivered. He ran back home. By this time Mother had started a fire outside. She did not laugh and talk as she usually did. Soon Nona came out. Then Father and at last Grandmother and Grandfather. Then Kemi heard Grandfather ask, "Is not *this* the day of the acorn gathering?"

"Yes," answered Father. "Some of us will go to the glen where the black oaks grow. Acorns are ripe."

Kemi was very happy. He could go too with his pal and cousin, Tonla. They would gather acorns together. Perhaps he would tell Tonla about the broken pot. It was hard to keep a secret. Perhaps Tonla could help. Anyway he would tell him.

19

CHAPTER 2: THE TREASURE

NOT ALL OF THE INDIANS of the Village among the Willows went acorn-gathering that beautiful morning. Grandmother was still weaving a small basket.

Grandfather wanted to stay home and help other old men weave a net to catch rabbits. As he wove he liked to tell stories of old days, if any one would listen—days when he was the great runner and knew the country near and far.

Mothers with very young babies stayed home. Some repaired the great storage bins, woven of willow branches, in which to store the new crop of acorns.

Of course there were always acorns to pound into flour. That never stopped. Between the huts were great rocks. Many had deep holes in them. These holes had been dug over the years by women who pounded acorns to a fine flour with a stone pestle. Other women

preferred to sit on the ground and pound acorns in a stone bowl called a mortar.

After the sun was up a small group of women, children and a few men led by Kemi's father started on a trail to the glen where the oak trees grew.

It was easy to follow the trail. It had been trod by the bare feet of Indians for years and years. Kemi and Tonla carried their rabbit sticks and empty baskets to fill with acorns. Each boy wore around his neck a bag of chia seeds. Chia seeds were good to eat, and growing boys are always hungry.

Father knew the trail. In fact, he knew every village in the great valley. Each village had borders that marked hunting and food gathering areas. No one ever thought of crossing into the area of another village. Perhaps that was *why* these Indians seldom quarrelled. There were very few battles among them. Such battles were usually about something that happened years ago and that everyone had forgotten. Not really serious battles, mostly name-calling.

Kemi and Tonla trotted behind Father. They watched and heard everything that moved. They heard woodpeckers drilling holes in the bark of dead trees. They heard quail calling to one another. They heard the warning barks of ground squirrels.

Suddenly Kemi saw high in the sky a great soaring eagle. The eagle scarcely flapped its wings but floated on air currents high above the earth. Kemi asked Father, "Do you think *that* eagle is the mother of the eagle we

have in the cage at home? I mean the one that belongs to the Headman who uses the feathers for sacred dances?"

His father smiled and answered, "It may well be. Do you see the nest high in that great tree over there?"

"Yes," said the boys in excitement. "It is big and old and way up."

"That is where the eagles raise their two or three eaglets every year," answered Father. "That is where we get but one eagle every year. We use the feathers in the sacred dances. You know, Kemi," he continued, "eagles always nest in the same place year after year. They build a new nest on top of the old one."

It had been the custom of these Indians for years, to whom the eagle was a sacred bird, to watch for the laying of the eggs in the nest. Then the chief of the village would send a boy to watch the growth of the young eagles. The boy had to climb a very high cliff nearby so he could look down from above.

After the eaglets began to grow feathers and were almost ready to leave the nest, a number of men climbed the tree. It was a dangerous thing to do, for grown eagles are very savage. But the men never took more than one young bird from the nest. They left the others to grow up.

It was a young eaglet which had been taken from this very nest that was now caged in the Village among the Willows. As the boys walked on, they saw the eagle soar out of sight and finally disappear.

Now they had reached the oak grove. As they crossed a little creek coming down from a hill Kemi stopped suddenly. "Look, Father! There. It is a grizzly bear's track in the mud."

As Wusi smelled the bear's track his hair stood up along his neck. He was afraid of bears too. But Father said calmly, "That is an old track. The bear feasted on acorns some suns ago. He is probably asleep somewhere in the hills. He will not bother us."

Indians hardly ever tried to kill a grizzly bear. Their stone arrowheads were too small and weak. The grizzly bear's hide and fur were tough and thick. Many grizzly bears roamed the hills and the river bottoms in those days. They were terrifying beasts. They were always angry and ready to attack. They were the masters of all life.

Long ago the Indians knew it was useless to try to kill a grizzly bear. So they came to believe that the bears *might* be their ancestors. They might have magic. They *might* be wizards. They might be men turned into bears.

Grandfather had once warned Kemi. He still remembered the warning.

"Little one," he had said, "I know you are as fleet as a deer, but if you should meet a grizzly bear do not run. Stand as still as a stick. Say quietly to the bear, 'I am your friend, Grandfather. I never said anything bad about you. I like you. I trust you.' Then the bear will walk away."

"I hope I never meet a bear when I am alone," whispered Kemi to his cousin. "They are so big. Their claws tear like knives."

"Well, the bear is gone," said Father. "Now we are at the grove."

The gathering of acorns began. Older children climbed the great oak trees and crawled out on spreading branches. As they swung the branches up and down acorns dropped to the ground like hail stones. Even the small children enjoyed hunting for acorns in the tall grasses. Baskets filled to overflowing. Nets bulged with acorns. It was a wonderful crop.

Some of the branches of the older trees were so heavy that they touched the ground. The boys climbed these great arms, jumping up and down as the acorns fell. Gray squirrels barked angrily. Jays screeched. Kemi saw a deer bound into the forest frightened by the noise.

By the time the sun was overhead every basket and net was full of acorns. The tired happy women sat on gray rocks laughing and talking and resting. Some of the young children slept.

But Kemi and Tonla were not tired at all. "Let's go rabbit hunting," said Kemi. "The people will not be going home until it gets cooler."

The boys wandered along the little creek keeping an eye out for bears. Wusi bounded ahead of them sniffing at every bush and hole, as dogs do. Then he smelled a ground squirrel in a hole and began to dig furiously. Dirt flew into the air. Wusi was very excited, but then he was *always* excited about hunting.

Suddenly something large and dark fell at Kemi's feet. At first he thought it was a rock. Then he saw it was an old leather bag; dirty, green with mold, and full of holes.

"Tonla, look! Come here. See what Wusi found," he called.

The boys opened the bag. The rotten leather draw string broke. Kemi spread out the bag. He gave a start of surprise. "Look, Tonla! A knife blade! Look at those arrowheads!" He held up a long, slender, clear knife blade. Tonla picked up some beautifully chipped arrowheads. There were also three balls of reddish and bluish stones, different from anything they had ever seen— shiny and clear.

As Kemi held the knife blade up to the sky he saw it was so clear he could almost see through it. The arrowheads were of the same clear stone. They were beautifully and carefully chipped. Both boys knew fine workmanship when they saw it. They *knew* arrowheads. They just sat on the ground and stared at the treasure.

"Who *could* have lost this bag? It's very old. Maybe somebody lost it a long time ago when he was hunting," said Tonla.

"It's full of holes. Maybe eaten by mice or pack rats."

"I think," said Kemi, staring at the strange treasure, "I think this bag has lain there a long time under leaves and grass. It cannot belong to anyone living today. We do not have stones like these around here."

He wiped the dirt from the knife blade. It shone as if it were polished. Meanwhile Wusi was still digging and whining, hoping to find the squirrel. He did not know what a great treasure he *had* discovered.

Suddenly Kemi looked thoughtfully at Tonla and said, "Now I must tell you something. I haven't told anybody. It's a secret. You must not tell anybody."

Tonla listened playing with the arrowheads. "Did you hear that Mother's soapstone bowl from the ocean had been broken to pieces by someone in the village?"

"Everybody knows that now. Of course I heard about it. My mother told me."

"Well," said Kemi sadly, "I broke the bowl. But don't tell anybody."

"*You!*" exclaimed Tonla.

"Yes, me," answered his friend. "But it just happened. I didn't *mean* to. I was sitting on the ground smoothing my rabbit stick. I saw a rabbit. I threw my stick at it! The stick bounced from a storage bin and struck the bowl hard—so hard it broke it all to pieces—bang!"

"And you never told anyone?"

"No. I was afraid to. I was afraid Father might tell the Headman. He might tell the Medicine Man. I am really afraid of the Medicine Man. Aren't you?"

"Of course I am. He's a wizard. You never know what he is going to do."

"I've been wondering," continued Kemi, "how I might get another cooking pot for Mother. But I have nothing to trade with. But these stones may be valuable. Perhaps Father may think so, too. Then, when he goes to the ocean to trade soon with the people who make the bowls, he *might* trade these for a new soapstone pot."

"That *is* an idea," answered Tonla.

"I will wait until tomorrow," answered Kemi, "and when Father is alone I will show him this bag. But I will have to tell him, then, that I was the one who broke the soapstone cooking pot."

"Yes, you will," answered his friend. "You *must*."

Wusi was still digging for the ground squirrel. He was still hoping to catch it. The boys wandered back to join the villagers. So Wusi *had* to follow them.

Soon everyone gathered up heavily loaded nets, bags and baskets, and started home. Even the little children carried something. It had been a wonderful day.

The people at home had mended the granaries which held acorns last year. Now once again they were getting full. No one would go hungry. It had almost always been so in this gracious land with these secure and happy people. There was always food for all.

CHAPTER 3: KEMI TELLS HIS FATHER

KEMI WAITED ANXIOUSLY the next morning for Father to be alone. Children were not allowed to talk to their elders when their elders were talking.

Father was helping the men of the village who were weaving a net of string made of milkweed fibers. Later in the fall they would peg this net down in some open place. The villagers would join together—men, women and children—and drive rabbits, squirrels, and quail toward the net. There they would be caught.

32

When the sun was high overhead and the day grew warm the men stopped weaving their net. Father wandered over to the shade of a tree near his hut to rest.

Many years ago when Father was young he, too, had been a messenger for the village. He, too, had carried messages from the Headman of his village to the Headman of some other village. Not only was he a very good runner but he had a good memory too. He had to remember every word of the message exactly as the Headman had told him. But now, years later, he no longer carried messages. That was for young people.

Father was resting in the shade of the tree his eyes closed. Kemi slipped into the hut, found the treasure bag under his sleeping mat. Then he came out and sat beside his father.

"Father," he said very quietly so that no one could hear him, "I want to show you something."

Father opened his eyes.

"Tonla and I found this yesterday near the Valley of the Oaks."

He handed Father the leather bag. As his father opened it and saw the strange beautiful stones his eyes widened in surprise. He breathed deeply as he stared at them. But he said nothing. He touched the stone knife blade. He handled the arrowheads. Then he looked at his son and asked, "Where did you find these, my son? They are old. They are rare. They may have been made by the Ancient Ones?"

Kemi answered, still very quietly. "Wusi, Tonla and

33

I were hunting for rabbits. Wusi smelled a ground squirrel or gopher in a hole. You know how excited he gets. He dug and whined and dug and whined. Finally, as we watched him, up flew this bag. When Tonla and I opened it we were so surprised. Are these *really* very valuable, Father?"

"Yes, my son. They are from the Old Ones. They are real treasures. Stone like this comes south *only* by trade. It comes from people who live far to the north near a lake, I am told. There is a great hill of this rock. Everybody wants some of it, of course. But we only get it by trading with other Indians."

He examined the bag carefully. He saw the holes eaten by field mice. He smelled the bag. He looked at the knife blade.

"This knife blade was chipped many years ago." Then he carefully studied the small arrowheads.

"Such fine work," he murmured under his breath.

"Now, Father," whispered Kemi, "I must tell you a secret."

"A secret? What is it you will tell me?" asked his father still handling the stone knife blade.

"Father, do you remember yesterday when Mother came home and found her soapstone pot broken to pieces?"

"Of course I do. It was *very* strange," said Father. Then he continued, "There was a crack in that bowl, at the mouth, but I mended it with tar. It has been a good pot. Mother has used it for years.

35

"Perhaps you do not know, but Grandfather was a great messenger in his day too. One fall he brought this pot from the ocean. He had traded with the People of the Mountains in the Sea who make these pots."

"Father, *I* broke that pot."

"You, Kemi?" asked his father in surprise.

Kemi shivered. He felt cold all over. He was so scared. But he went on with the story.

"It happened this way. I was sitting right here where we sit now, smoothing my new rabbit stick. I saw a rabbit under a bush. I threw my stick at it, but the stick hit a storage bin over there. As it bounced back, it just happened to strike Mother's pot on the ground very hard. The pot broke to pieces. I didn't *mean* to do it."

Kemi's father's eyes looked angry. He *was* angry.

"Why didn't you tell us? I heard Mother weeping during the night. You must know, son, that soapstone pots like these are very hard to get. Few women in the village own them—especially one as fine as hers was."

"I know, Father," answered Kemi softly, almost in tears. "I did not tell because I was afraid. I was afraid you would tell the Headman. Then he might tell the Medicine Man or the Bear Man. I am afraid of him. He makes people well, they say, but also he makes them sick. He has *magic*. I've never forgotten how the Bear Man looks with the great hide and bear's head and claws and sharp white teeth."

"I understand that," answered his father. "Many of us are afraid of the Medicine Man, but often he cures peo-

37

ple's sickness. He knows more than we do. He knows all about herbs and leaves and charms that will make people well."

"Father, that was just the reason I did not tell you. I was afraid. I have heard of some boys who have been beaten with sharp nettles."

"Most of that talk is just idle talk," answered Father. "We would understand that it was an accident. But I am glad you told me at last."

"Father, since I found the old bag with the rare stones I have been wondering about something else."

"What is it now?"

"Soon you will go to the ocean to trade. You always go in the fall. I know the People of the Mountains in the Sea sometimes bring soapstone pots when they come in their great boats. Do you think, Father, that they might like these old arrowheads and this sharp knife blade? Do you think we might trade these for a new bowl for Mother?"

"Oh!" sighed Father. "So that is your idea!"

Kemi somehow knew that his father wanted the knife blade for himself. His own knife was old and worn. But his father said nothing for a long time. Kemi waited patiently. After a while he asked again.

"Father, if you *do* go to the ocean to trade, and you think the stones are valuable, may I go with you? I have never been to the ocean."

He saw the expression on his father's face change. It grew very thoughtful.

39

"It is a long trip to the ocean, my son. Many times in my youth as a messenger I have gone to the ocean. In some places it is dangerous. Grizzly bears hide in the tangled brush of the river. There are swamps to cross. You have to know the trail across the river near the ocean. The cattails and tule are so high you can hardly see the sky. And there are many rattlesnakes. I will have to think about this. I cannot answer today. It is a long way for a young boy like you to walk."

"Yes, Father. But I am a very fast runner, you know. At the time when the boys race in honor of Wyot and the new moon, I am usually first."

"Yes, I hear," answered Father. "It *may* be when you are older and taller you will be a runner and messenger like your grandfather and myself. If you ever *do* become a messenger you have to learn all about the country around us. You have to learn every trail, every creek, and where the dangers are. I must think about this. I must talk to the Headman. Perhaps in a day or so I will let you know. I, too, would like Mother to have a new cooking pot. It would make her very happy. The mush would cook quicker. But we must wait."

Kemi knew the talk was over. Father took the bag and put it among his stone tools. Kemi had hid the three balls for himself. One was reddish and two were bluish. He had not shown them to Father. But now he would just have to wait until Father made up his mind.

It seemed to Kemi that the next two days would just *never* end. He waited and waited for Father to speak to

40

him. He watched Father enter the Headman's hut the next morning and stay there a long time. He saw Father talking to the Medicine Man also. Yet another day passed and Father did not say anything.

Finally on the third day Father called Kemi to him. He sat down on the ground in the shade of a tree. Kemi waited.

After a quiet time his father said, "Son, I have talked to the elders. They have been watching you for a long time. They have seen that you are swift of foot. They know that you have often been first in the races at the new moon time. And a few years from now, if you should become a messenger for the village, you will need to know about the country around us. Now we must know if you have a good memory too. I have talked with the Headman and the Medicine Man. They both believe it might be good for you to go with us to the ocean."

Kemi gave a great sigh. He saw his father smile. He knew his father was happy, too.

"Father, I promise to be quiet and not complain if I get hungry or tired. And I will carry a load, too. But then, Father," he said, "I will be all alone with the big men. I am not *yet* a man. Do you think it would be better if Tonla, my cousin, could go too? We are good friends. We could help you. We could *both* carry loads."

Kemi saw his father hesitate. But then it always took Father so long to make up his mind. After a while Father said, "Perhaps it might be better to have your cousin

along. You would be happier. And each one of you could carry your share of the load." He stood up and went over to the little sweathouse perhaps to talk things over with Grandfather.

Kemi ran through the village until he found Tonla. Tonla was skinning a rabbit he had just killed. Talking very quietly so no else could hear, he said, "Tonla, Father says I can go to the ocean when the men go to trade. And you can go, too."

"Oh!" exclaimed Tonla. "Let's climb our tree and talk about it."

He finished skinning and cleaning his rabbit. He gave it to his mother. Then the boys climbed their favorite sycamore tree. They talked together the rest of the day about the wonderful journey ahead of them.

CHAPTER 4: TO THE SEA

BEFORE DAWN, several days later, six men and two boys from the Village among the Willows were on the trail. Each one was heavily loaded down with trade goods. They carried deer hides, deer antlers, bundles of dried venison, berries, pine nuts, acorns, and other foods from the great valley.

Father led the group for he knew the trail best. The boys knew they would get very hungry and tired. Father had warned them it would be so. But as they straggled above the river, as it wound for hours and hours through the valley, they found it hard to keep up with the men.

The Indians traveled with a steady trot, their heads bent forward. It seemed easier to carry heavy burdens this way. No one stopped to rest, to eat, or even talk.

At last as the sun was sinking, Father said, "Let us camp for the night under that sycamore tree by the river. You have done well, boys."

Everyone was happy to unload his heavy pack and lie down on the solid earth. Someone made a fire with his fire sticks. They had killed several rabbits during the afternoon and soon the odor of baking rabbits filled the air. It was cooler now.

After eating, the travelers rested in a group and talked while the boys listened. They talked mostly of the day to come and when they would get to the ocean. They spoke of the dangers of meeting grizzly bears. For they had to cross the river before it reached the ocean. That was a dangerous place. When they once got across the river to the Village on the Little Hill overlooking the ocean, Father would find his old friend Tula. There they would camp.

Usually after eating, the travelers played a game with marked sticks. But tonight they were too tired. Everyone rolled up in his rabbit skin blanket and was soon fast asleep.

Coyotes yipped from the hillside. A gray fox nosed the camp and disappeared like a shadow. A grizzly bear may have prowled in the brush along the river. The moon rose and set. The night wore on.

Morning came so suddenly it seemed to Kemi that he had just fallen asleep. But before dawn everyone had bathed in the river, eaten cold cakes of acorn mush and was on the trail. Kemi walked beside his father. Once, as they stopped for a moment, his father said, "Son, be sure to look at everything. Try to remember the trail and where the river turns and twists. If you ever become a

messenger for the village you *must* know and remember every place in the great valley."

So Kemi looked and remembered. The day wore on. Then, at a turn in the trail, he noticed a huge rock. In the shadow of the rock he saw a coiled rattlesnake.

"Father, look! A rattlesnake!"

Everyone stopped.

A large bird, a roadrunner, was dancing back and forth before the coiled rattlesnake. Just as the snake struck at the bird, the bird jumped into the air. Then he pranced back and forth, teasing the rattlesnake, which struck again and again.

Since roadrunners lived mostly on lizards and snakes, the Indians knew this would be a fight and the roadrunner would be the victor. They crouched on the ground and watched.

The snake struck again and again at the bird. Its fangs were dripping with poison. But, each time, it struck only an outstretched wing feather—nothing more—never the body of the bird. Back and forth, back and forth the roadrunner danced, trailing a wing on the ground and *daring* the snake to strike. But the snake was getting tired. It was losing its poison. The bird knew this.

With a quick swish of a wing, the roadrunner brushed sand into the snake's eyes. The snake has no eyelids, so it was blinded. Then the roadrunner jumped on its back and struck time and time again with his sharp bill. Soon the snake was lifeless.

Now that the snake was dead, the great bird began to swallow it head first. And he scampered away into the brush, dragging the snake's long tail behind him.

To the Indians of this time, rattlesnakes, like ravens, swordfish and dolphins, were sacred. Some Indians believed the rattlesnake saw everything good or bad that men did. They believed snakes carried messages to the Creator of All Life, so they rarely harmed them.

Now the traders rose and trotted westward. A fog slowly drifted in from the ocean, covering hills and valleys like a faint smoke. Kemi saw seabirds drifting in the fog and wind. They made strange, wild cries. Suddenly he noticed a hut half hidden in the fog. He heard dogs barking. Father said, "We are passing a village called the Village of the Old Houses. We do not know these people, but we speak their language."

Soon after they passed the village they heard the

shouting and yelling of many people. One of the traders said, "The People of the Old Houses must be having a rabbit hunt." Soon the sounds of shouting faded away.

"Tonla," said Kemi, "taste the air. It's salty on the tongue."

Tonla answered, "It *does* taste salty. We must be nearing the ocean."

And soon their keen young ears heard a far-off steady boom-boom, like thunder far away.

"What is that boom-boom-boom, Father? It sounds like a coming storm. When Takis is angry and sends lightning and thunder to frighten us. It sounds like Takis."

Father laughed. "That is not Takis, my son. That is the sound the ocean always makes. It never stops. When we do get to the ocean if the fog is gone you will see water, water, water, to the very end of the world. Nothing but water. Waves always pounding on the rocks and sand, boom-boom-boom. Day and night.

"But, before we can reach the Village on the Little Hill where my friend Tula is Headman, we will have to cross the river. This is the most dangerous part of the trip."

It *was* a dangerous place. It was where the waters spread. The river divided into many channels. It was a jungle. Willows grew there. The reeds and the rushes were higher than a man's head. There were very few trails through this thick growth.

Even with the slippery trail, the giant grasses, the

deep pools of water, it *still* would have taken the traders a long time to cross.

Suddenly the boys, with their keen eyes, saw something moving upstream.

Kemi whispered to Father quietly, "Father, look over there, under the wild grape vines."

Then all of the traders saw a mother grizzly bear and her cubs. She had been eating wild grapes under an alder tree.

It was well that the wind blew away from the traders toward the sea. The mother bear did not smell them. She had been too busy eating grapes.

Now all the men were frightened. There was nothing more dangerous than a grizzly bear with cubs. They all stopped. They stood quietly, not moving on the slippery trail. They hardly breathed. A long time passed.

Finally the mother bear ambled slowly up-stream followed by her cubs. They saw her no more.

The traders sighed with relief. But there *might* be other grizzly bears hidden in the dense swamp. They must still walk carefully and watch carefully.

At last they reached the other side of the river. Now they were safe. They climbed a hill. They could hear dogs barking and children shouting. They smelled the sea. They had finally reached the Village on the Little Hill.

"We will camp here near the village," said Father. "I will find my friend Tula who is Headman. If the fog lifts tonight you can see far." He left them.

53

Kemi could not see anything because of the dense fog. But the boys heard people talking all around them. They unloaded their heavy packs.

As they lay on the ground they listened to the pounding of the surf. The cries of the seabirds were shrill to their ears. They smelled strange new smells—seaweed, fish, salt water. They rested.

After a while Father returned with his friend. Kemi heard Father ask Tula, "Have the traders from the Mountains in the Sea come to trade?"

"They were here some suns ago," answered Tula. "If the fog goes away and the sea is quiet they may come soon again."

As the traders talked with Tula the boys found a soft place in the sand out of the wind. They nibbled chia seeds and acorn cakes. But they were too sleepy and tired to listen to man-talk. They snuggled together in the soft sand. The boom-boom of the surf and the shrill cries of the sea gulls lulled them to sleep.

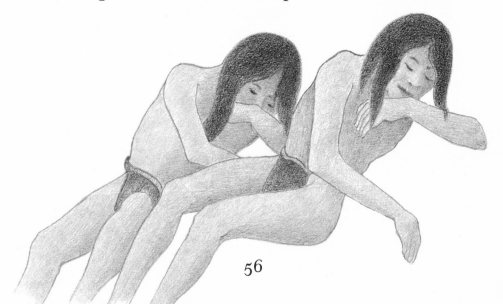

CHAPTER 5: THE WHALE

IT WAS A GOOD NIGHT to sleep. Sea, sky, and rocks were hidden in a blanket of fog. Cooking fires died down. Dogs stopped barking. Only the surf kept up its restless moaning.

But after midnight the fog drifted slowly out to sea. The sky became clear. No one was awake. No one saw the half-moon lighting up the crests of the waves as they crashed over rocks. No one saw the lazy surf creeping up the sand in the moonlight like a white ribbon. And so the long night went by slowly.

Just before dawn Kemi awoke with a sudden start. He heard a strange sound. Where was he? He sat up and then he remembered where he was. He was at the sea.

Over there under that tree lay Father and the village traders, sound asleep. As he looked out over the sea he saw nothing but water, water, water to the end of the world. The waves never stopped. The surf boom-boomed like thunder. How *could* there be so much water? Did the world *never* end?

Once again he heard the strange sounds that had awakened him. They were like the growls of the Bear Man in the village at ceremonial time. The Bear Man frightened people, all people, old and young, with his bear robe and bear head, sharp teeth and growls.

Kemi, still half asleep, heard more frightening growls. He looked up-shore and saw a long, dark, smooth thing in the breaking surf. It looked like a huge smooth rock. The strange sounds seemed to come from that rock. As he watched he saw dark moving animals. What could they be? They sounded like grizzly bears.

Kemi was frightened. He shook his cousin. "Tonla, wake up!"

"What is it?" Tonla was angry at being awakened. "Where am I? I'm cold. It's dark." Tonla wanted to snuggle back into his rabbit skin blanket.

"We're at the sea, Tonla, with Father. Don't you re-member? Wake up! Listen! Hear bears growling?"

Tonla listened. "They sound like the Medicine Man at home," he said. He was now wide awake. "Where are the bears, Kemi?" he whispered.

"See that big rock there at the water's edge way up there? See those dark animals moving around the rock?

They *must* be bears. Smell the terrible smell? We must wake up Father! If they are *really* grizzly bears everyone in the villages must know."

Kemi stumbled in the darkness to the mound of sleeping men. He found Father and gently touched his shoulder. Father was a light sleeper.

"Why do you waken me in the middle of the night?" he said angrily. "I'm tired. *Now* what is the matter?"

"We are afraid, Father. There are animals along the ocean. They growl like bears. Come and see."

At the word BEARS Father woke up. He, too, was afraid of grizzly bears. Rubbing his eyes, he straggled to the edge of the hill and looked where Kemi pointed. The moon lit up the ocean and shore.

"There is a dead whale over there in the surf!" Father exclaimed. "The bears have come from their lairs among the tules in the river we crossed yesterday." He became excited.

"But, Father, how could a great whale get caught in the sand? He is as long as our village! I never saw anything as big as that!"

"The whale may have been lost," answered Father. "Perhaps our friends, the swordfish, drove him to the shore. There is enough whale to feed all the villagers along the coast. I will wake up Tula. He must know at once. He is a Headman. He will know how to drive the bears away."

Father entered the Headman's hut. Meanwhile the boys listened to the angry bears and shivered with fear.

Before long everybody knew about the stranded whale. They poured from their homes as news passed from hut to hut, village to village. Perhaps a thousand people lived in the villages along the coast at that time. We do not really know. Later the Spanish named it the Bay of Smokes from the smoke of the many village fires they saw.

Kemi heard Tula say, "We will drive the bears away with fire. They fear only fire."

People gathered dry reeds and made torches. The reeds burned quickly. Then the most courageous men walked slowly along the seashore toward the great bulk of the whale. They shouted and yelled and sang as they marched with their flaming torches. The grizzly bears were still tearing greedily at the dead whale.

Kemi and Tonla sat on a sandy knoll and watched. They were afraid to get too close to the terrible beasts as the smell of the dead whale spread everywhere.

As the Indians, holding their torches, came near the whale, the bears slowly backed away. They may have been eating on the whale for a long time and were not very hungry. But they were *very* afraid of fire. Snarling and angry, they ambled toward the tangled river-bed which was their lair. They would hide there and sleep during the day.

This whale was the largest the Indians had seen stranded in the sand for many years. Now more and more excited Indians poured from their huts. The Headmen of the villages called the Dividers of the Food to come with their sharp stone knives and sharp reeds to cut the whale to pieces and divide it equally among all the people.

Now the Indians started fires along the shore and before their huts. Women brought nets and skins to drag bloody hunks of meat to fires. The great whale was hacked to pieces, by the Dividers of the Food. Whale meat must be cooked quickly for it soon spoils.

Kemi and Tonla soon smelled a better smell—the odor of roasting whale. Indians, like bears, liked nothing better than roasted whale.

Village dogs dived between people's legs grabbing scraps. Gulls swooped down to steal bits of meat, then whirled away to some safe rock to eat it. Black ravens flew on the carcass, too. But ravens were sacred to the Indians. No one chased them away.

In late afternon nothing remained of the great whale but towering white ribs and bones. From these bones the Indians would later carve spears, hair ornaments, and tools to pry shellfish from rocks, or even use ribs for starting a new hut.

The sand where the whale had died was dark red with blood. But the night tide would carry away the stain. In the morning the sand would be white again.

Now the tide was going out. Rocks that had been covered with water that morning now stood high above the breakers.

Kemi and Tonla wandered along the beach watching dogs, birds and people, and talking to the children.

67

The tide left water in holes among the rocks. These were tide pools. Kemi and Tonla spent much of the afternoon exploring the tide pools.

Now they found a new friend, Yoko. Yoko was the son of a Headman of a village. Of course he had lived all his life along the sea. He knew about shells, birds, and the dangers of the great ocean. He was older than Kemi and Tonla, almost a man.

"Look! There!" said Kemi, pointing at a purple flower growing under the water in a tide pool. The flower had long feelers swaying in the water.

"What a funny flower," said Tonla, "growing *under* the water."

"That's not a flower," laughed Yoko. "That's an animal. It eats fish."

"It *can't* be an animal," said Tonla stoutly. "It's a flower."

"You just watch," said his friend. "Watch that tiny fish there. If it touches one of those swaying feelers see what happens—"

They watched, hardly daring to breathe. A tiny fish touched a waving feeler of the flower. At once all of the other feelers wrapped themselves around the fish. Soon the fish disappeared in a hole, the mouth of a sea anemone. The inland boys were amazed.

"It looks like a flower but acts like an animal," said Kemi.

"It's *both*," answered Tonla.

Yoko showed them another strange animal shaped like a star. It moved along slowly under the water. It had a rough red skin.

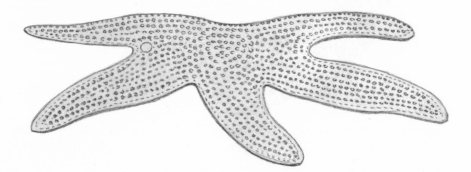

"That's a starfish," said their friend. "There's lots of them in the pools. Many colors, too. They can live out of the water or in the water." Yoko felt proud of his knowledge. Of course he was older and wiser.

Then Yoko pointed to a small red animal crawling over the sand. It had but one big claw. It was a crab. It walked sideways but never forward as other animals did.

"They are good to eat," was all that Yoko said.

Kemi and Tonla saw many plants and animals they had never known. They were not sure whether each new one was a plant or animal. Some had many sharp spines on them like the fruit of the cactus they knew so well.

"I'll show you some shells to take home," said Yoko.

He led them to the beach where high tide had left many shells on the sand. The boys would have liked to have carried *all* of them home. They were each so different and so beautiful in color.

Kemi ran back to camp to get an empty net to carry home as many shells as he could. He knew Mother and Nona would like them.

Kemi also gathered bits of black tar he found at the water's edge. Father always needed tar to mend all kinds of tools and jars. Mother used tar to line jar-shaped water jugs.

The boys saw a sea gull dig a clamshell from the sand. Then the bird flew into the air and dropped the shell on the rocks below. He knew the shell would break.

Before the clever gull could dive to grab the tasty clam another gull glided below him and stole the clam.

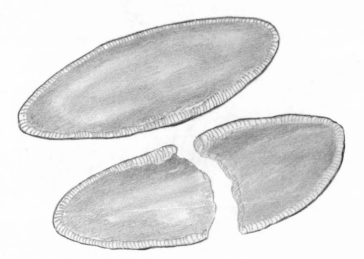

Then on a rock where huge waves broke furiously they saw a strange bird. It had a long bag under its bill. It was a pelican.

They watched the pelican dive into the sea and catch a fish. It flew back to a rock and *seemed* to swallow the fish. But the fish really slipped into the bag.

"When the pelican gets very hungry," said Yoko, "it coughs up a fish and then really swallows it. The bag is just a place to store it."

By now the boys were tired. So much had happened since early morning. They lay on the sand and just looked. Finally Kemi, pointing to a small rocky island not far away, asked Yoko, "What's on that island over there?"

"Oh, that's a bad place," answered Yoko. "Lots of rattlesnakes are on that island."

"Why are there so many snakes on *that* island?" asked the boys.

"In the winter come great floods. Many rattlesnakes live in the river bottom where you crossed yesterday. The snakes are carried out to sea and swim to that island."

The boys shivered. They were *afraid* of rattlesnakes.

After resting they swam out to a big rock high above the breakers and climbed on it. Looking toward the great dark island, Kemi asked his friend, "Do you think traders will come soon to trade?"

Yoko answered, "If the sea is quiet and there is no fog they may come. One *never* knows.

"Those people over there have fine plank boats like ours, not like boats of reeds that we paddle around in on the river. Big, strong boats that hold twenty men. The island people come only when they need something from us."

And so the long afternoon passed away. The sun was setting, making the ocean red as if it were burning up.

Feasting went on for hours and hours. After the feasting was all over the time came to honor the friendly swordfish. The Indians believed that swordfish had driven the whale to its death. They believed that the swordfish was their friend. So were dolphins. Dolphins guarded their world from harm and thus were never harmed.

Only one dancer celebrated the dance of the swordfish. But everybody joined, clapping their hands, stomping their feet, singing and chanting the honor of the swordfish. Shells filled with stones and cemented with pitch were clanged to the rhythm of the singing and dancing.

The costume of the swordfish dancer was beautiful. From his head projected the long bony sword from a real swordfish. The cap on his head also covered part of his back. It was made of shining sea shells shaped like the scales of a fish.

His dance was more like the swimming of a fish than dancing. It was an exciting dance to watch. He told in dance the story of the battle of the swordfish and the whale. The songs the Indians sang in his honor were

beautiful. But slowly, as the night wore on, one child after another fell asleep.

At last even Kemi and Tonla could not stay awake. Full of whale meat and tired by all they had done during the day, they crept to their sleeping place and covered themselves with rabbit skin blankets. As Kemi fell asleep the last thing he said to Tonla was, "I wonder if the traders *will* come tomorrow. The fog is gone. I wonder if Father still has the knife and arrowheads in his bag with his tools."

CHAPTER 6: THE TRADERS

A S KEMI LOOKED out over the sea the next morning he noticed something small and dark on the water far away. The sky was clear. He could see the dark something moving slowly toward the mainland. It could not be a whale, a seal, or a dolphin because it did not vanish.

Sometimes it disappeared for a moment as a great wave rose and fell in the ocean. But as he watched it grew larger. IT MUST BE A BOAT! Father and Tonla were watching too.

"How long does it take a boat to come from the island, Father?"

"That depends upon the waves and the tide. Sometimes the water is very rough. Sometimes the tide is going out and it is hard to paddle against it. But I *do* think that *is* the traders' boat."

"How many men are in the boat, Father?" asked Kemi.

Father watched the boat as it grew larger and answered, "There may be five or six men. I cannot tell from this distance. Usually they bring a boy along to bail water from the boat. Often it leaks. Sometimes the waves are high."

"Oh," thought Kemi. "There may be a boy in the boat from the island." He was curious about him. Did he look and talk like all other boys? What kind of people lived on the island? After all they were *strangers*.

"Father," he asked, "do the people of the island look like us? I'm a little afraid of them. People say strange things about them. Some say they are wizards. Others say they know more than we do. Are they to be feared, Father?"

"My son," said Father in his quiet voice, "these people are *not* strangers. They speak as we do. We know what they say. They know what we say. They come as friends to trade with us. Tula says he has traded with them for many years. He says they are very wise in many ways. He says they know more things about the Creator of Life and animals than we know. Grandfather says so too.

"But you have to watch out for them when you trade

79

with them," he said smiling. "They are clever traders. You sit behind us on the sand and watch and learn. These people like to sit all day and bargain. A little less, a little more. Sometimes they get more from us than we want to give them. They are keen."

"Father," said Kemi, "I hope they like our beautiful old arrowheads and our stone knife. I hope they have soapstone bowls with them."

"They usually bring many things when they come. Things we need and the people who live along the ocean need. They bring big roots that are very good when they are baked. They bring seal skins softer than rabbit fur. But it cost so much in trade for those fine furs. They bring pipes of soapstone; and bone flutes with several holes and fishhooks of shining abalone shell."

"Well, I hope," sighed Kemi, "that they bring a cooking pot to trade for our arrowheads."

"They will," said Father with confidence. "If these rare stones are valuable to us they will want them too."

The boat was coming nearer and nearer. Now many of the villagers had come from their huts and were watching the incoming boat. They liked the traders from the islands to come. Trading made a long and exciting day. It was a change for everyone.

At last Kemi counted six men in the oncoming boat and one boy. The boy was dipping water from the stern of the boat as great waves splashed over it.

The time had come for Father and his friends to carry the trading goods down to the shore. They spread out

deer hides on the sand and laid on them piles of acorns, dried berries, deer skins, deer antlers and other things they had brought from home. They sat down and waited. The boys sat behind the men. Children were not allowed to trade. They must watch quietly and learn by watching.

As the long boat slid through the pounding surf, missing sharp rocks, the traders jumped out and dragged it up on the sand. The boys saw that it was a very long boat. It was made of short planks of wood tied together with plant fibers. All the holes were filled with black tar to keep the water out. They were like Yoko's father's boat.

After they had made the boat safe the traders from the island carried their wares covered with sealskin and placed them on the sand. Trading began.

As Kemi watched these men talking and laughing, he saw that they looked just like other Indians. They talked the same. They laughed the same. They *were* the same.

Trading was a great game. It would last all day. Village people stood around and watched. Which side would get the better of the other? A trader would add a little more of this or that and try to seal the bargain. Sometimes it was not enough. The other trader would ask for more.

But there was no hurry. The longer it took to trade the more fun it was. So the game went on and on. Nobody wanted to stop.

Kemi saw a few pieces of soapstone carvings lying on the seal skin. There was a bone flute with three holes; some pipes, a small carved dolphin and a very tiny soapstone bowl.

"Do you think they have any cooking pots, Father? I don't see any," he whispered.

"We will wait and see," answered Father. "There may be one or two in the boat hidden under a seal skin."

Time passed. Acorns were traded and bags of pine nuts; dried venison changed hands. The traders of the island took all the deer antlers Father had brought from home. Deer antlers were good tools. Especially in making boats. All the deer skins were traded too.

On Father's deer skin lay a huge pile of roots; some shining abalone shells, lovely as a sunset; a few shiny fishhooks; a pipe for Grandfather and strings of shells for Mother and Nona.

It was late afternoon. One of the traders walked back to the boat. He took out something. Kemi saw it was a pot 'soapstone. The trader laid it down. Father looked at 1 It was handsome. Now it was Father's turn to offer something. *Now* was the time! He held up one of the fine clear arrowheads.

The island trader gave a little gasp of surprise. He took the arrowhead and looked it over carefully. Father heard him whisper to one sitting next to him, "Very fine, very old." Father pointed to the cooking pot but the traders from the island said "No."

Father now took out a larger arrowhead. Again the

island trader shook his head. The bartering was on in earnest.

It was a long, long game. Father added his last bag of pine nuts and chia seeds. Then there was more silence. No one said anything. The trader from the island knew that Father wanted that pot very much so he was going to get all he could! It was beautifully carved.

Father saw that he would have to give more. At last, unhappily, he took the long shining stone knife from the bag. He really hoped to have it for himself. He held it up. The island trader gave a sudden gasp of surprise. He took the knife blade. He felt its sharp edge. He held it up to the sky. It was a *perfect* knife blade. Both men knew it. How he wanted it!

The island trader knew that the knife blade was old and had come from far away. Again there was a long silence. The people watched. Somehow they knew that the trading was over. The island trader pointed to the bowl. Then he said to Father, "It is yours." And he took the knife blade, smiling.

By now the sun was sinking into the ocean. The boys smelled fish baking. The rancid smell of the dead whale was still strong.

The day was ended. Kemi was happy. He had at last gotten his wish.

The sea had become rough and angry. The people from the island did not dare to venture into it. They must stay overnight.

After the trading was over, Kemi, Tonla and Yoko

talked with the boy from the island. He was the son of a village Headman. Since he spoke the same language they could talk about many things—fish, seals, octopus, birds, and their families.

As they became friends the island boy showed Kemi a little whale carved of soapstone. Its eyes were beautiful. They were carved circles of sea shell set into the stone but the tail had been broken off. As soon as he saw it Kemi wanted that whale. If he could *only* get it!

But would the boy like anything *he had*? He took from the treasure bag under his belt some bright blue and red feathers he once had found—the feathers of birds near home. The boy said no. Feathers were not enough. Every boy gathered bright bird feathers.

Now Kemi thought of the balls of obsidian he had kept out for himself. One was red and two were the color of sea.

The boy from the island could not resist these colored stones. He smiled and handed Kemi the whale with the shell eyes. Now Kemi was indeed happy. He would love to take the whale home. Now he would tell all his many cousins in the village the story of the *big* whale.

It was growing cold. Fog was creeping in from the ocean. Since the traders from the valley were to leave before dawn the boys bedded down in the sand early. Kemi clutched his tailless whale with the seashell eyes and slept.

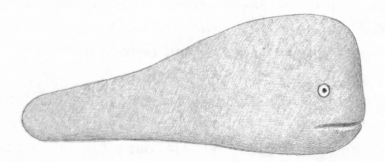

CHAPTER 7: HOME AGAIN

FOR SOME REASON it did not *seem* to take as long to get home as to go to the ocean. Of course it was always slow crossing the dangerous river channel, looking out for rattlesnakes and bears. But after they got on the firm old trail once more everybody trotted fast.

Ocean fog had crept once more inland for miles and miles. The traders saw the great mountains beyond their village a long time before they came near home. The weather must have changed while they were away. Even patches of snow were on the highest mountain peaks.

But at last they came nearer the Village among the Willows. They could hear the dogs barking. The boys had carried the precious cooking pot wrapped in a deer skin all the way home. It had been very heavy.

Now everybody rushed out to welcome them and to see what they had brought. Father gave Mother and Nona strings of shells. He brought Grandfather a carved soapstone pipe which he *had* to smoke at once.

Even though the ocean had been wonderful and a new world, still Kemi and Tonla were happy when they sat down around the fire inside the hut. Father talked and talked. He told about the battle between the roadrunner and the snake. He told a long story about Kemi and his discovery of the whale. He made a great exciting story of how the people of the seacoast drove away the grizzly bears with fire.

Father gave Grandmother some of the big roots from the island to bake. Finally he said, "Son, what have you under that deer skin that was so heavy to carry? I *thought* you brought something for your Mother."

Now came Kemi's *greatest* moment. He unwrapped the skin from around the bowl and placed the bowl on the ground before his Mother. "This is for you, Mother. Tonla and I carried it all the way from the ocean. It was very heavy. We traded for it. It was the most beautiful one that the island people had."

Mother's eyes opened in wide surprise. Tears rolled down her cheeks. She touched the bowl as if it were something sacred, as if it were something she had never hoped to have again. She turned it around and around studying the design the island artist had carved around it.

"It is beautiful, my son," she sighed. "It is more beautiful than the one that was broken—almost *too* beautiful to cook in."

Then, turning to her husband, she said smiling, "You will eat your mush more quickly, my husband. It will not be sour either as it was in the old granite pot."

She put her arms around Kemi and he felt very near to her. Now Grandmother put her arms around him too. He felt he was *really* at home.

Then he took from his little bag the small soapstone whale.

Kemi's father had already told the story of the whale. Now Kemi had to tell it over again in his *own* way. He had to tell how he had discovered it. He told of the beautiful dance of the swordfish and the strange costume that the dancer wore.

As they were about ready to go to bed, Kemi lay by his Mother and whispered, "Mother, I must tell you something. I must tell you how your bowl got broken. I never told you but I told Father. I happened to break it when I threw my stick at a rabbit."

"Oh!" was all she said.

"I never told you either," he whispered, "how Tonla and I found an old bag with some fine obsidian arrowheads and a beautiful stone knife in it. They were very rare.

"That is one reason Father let me go to the ocean. Some day, Mother, I may be a messenger like Father and Grandfather. Then I will have to *know all* of the country about us, the trails, the rivers, and how to go to the sea. I will tell you more about it tomorrow. I'm so tired now my legs hurt."

"Son, we will talk about it tomorrow. But I am so happy to get the bowl that I cannot say anything but that I am happy. It is almost *too* beautiful!"

Grandfather, Grandmother, and Father were already sound asleep.

Kemi found his own sleeping mat and was soon asleep. In one hand he held the little tailless soapstone whale with the shining shell eyes. He dreamed of whales, sea birds and the swordfish dance. And the wonderful plant-animals in the tide pools. The sea world was beautiful and strange. Still it was good to be home in his own hut with his own family. When he was older and a messenger he would go again to the great ocean.

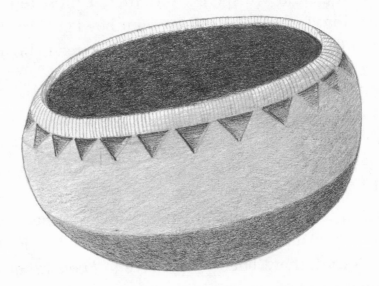